# Child War Refugees

Petrice Custance

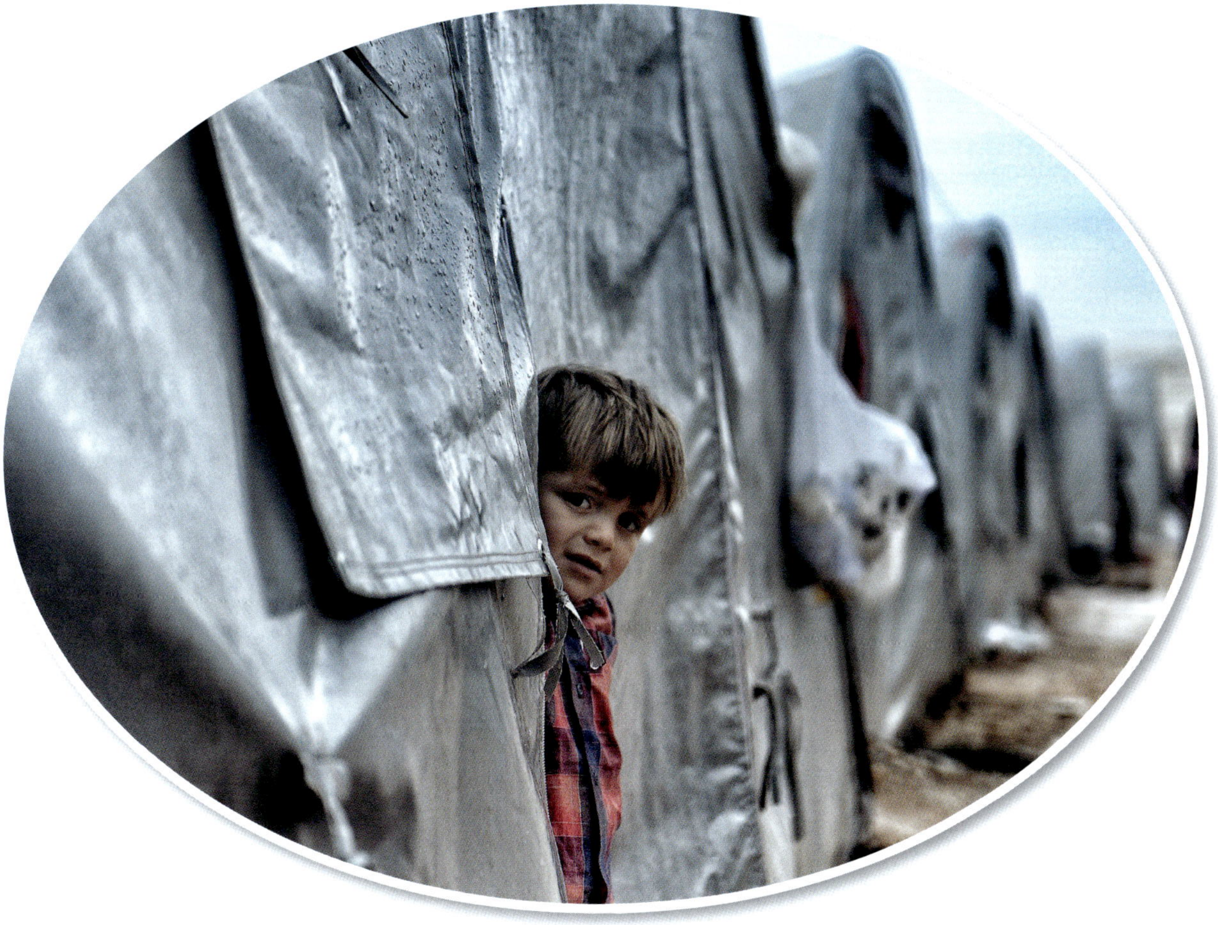

**A Crabtree Forest Book**

**Author:** Petrice Custance

**Series research and development:**
Ellen Rodger and Janine Deschenes

**Editorial director:** Kathy Middleton

**Editor:** Ellen Rodger and Janine Deschenes

**Proofreader:** Melissa Boyce

**Design:** Samara Parent

IMAGE CREDITS

**Shutterstock:**
Anas-Mohammed: p 31; Andrea Raffin: p 45 (top); Anjo Kan: p 22; Anton_Ivanov: p 9 (bottom); Art Babych: p 39; Bascar: p42 (bottom); ChameleonsEye: p 37 (middle); David Peinado Romero: p 16–17 (both); Drop of Light: p 7, 33, 42–43 (top); Everett Collection: p 6, 9 (top), 8 (bottom), 11 (middle), 13, 18, 19 (bottom); Fishman64: p 37 (top); GiuseppeCrimeni: p 12 (bottom); hikrcn: p 5 (top), 10–11, 36; lev radin: p 28 (bottom); Mohammad Bash: p 26 (bottom), 34; Mykola Tys: p 41; Nelson Antoine: p 21; Nicolas Economou: front cover; Pazargic Liviu: p 32; Peter Braakmann: p 40 (bottom); Philip Robinson 1: p 45 (bottom); quetions123: title page, p 5 (bottom); Richard Juilliart: p 4, 43 (middle), 44; Ryan Rodrick Beiler: p 30 (both); Sk Hasan Ali: p 26–27 (top); Stacey Newman: p 40 (top); svic: p 8 (top); Tolga Sezgin: p 35; Trent Inness: p 24 (bottom); Vic Hinterlang: p 14–15 (both); ZouZou: p 38

**Wikimedia Commons:**
Plenz: p 23; public domain: p 12 (top), 19 (top), 20, 24–25, 28–29

---

**Crabtree Publishing**

crabtreebooks.com 800-387-7650

In Canada: We acknowledge the financial support of the Government of Canada through the Canada Book Fund for our publishing activities.

Hardcover 978-1-0398-1528-5
Paperback 978-1-0398-1554-4
Ebook (pdf) 978-1-0398-1606-0
Epub 978-1-0398-1580-3

**Published in Canada**
**Crabtree Publishing**
616 Welland Avenue
St. Catharines, Ontario
L2M 5V6

**Published in the United States**
**Crabtree Publishing**
347 Fifth Avenue
Suite 1402-145
New York, New York, 10016

**Library and Archives Canada Cataloguing in Publication**
Available at Library and Archives Canada

**Library of Congress Cataloging-in-Publication Data**
Available at the Library of Congress

Printed in the U.S.A./072023/CG20230214

# CONTENTS

# Introduction

"Water is made of hydrogen and oxygen..." Zahra is studying science in the tent she shares with her brother in the refugee camp they have lived in for more than two years. Zahra and Yunus are alone in the world. Their parents, sister, and grandmother were killed when missiles hit their apartment building. Zahra and Yunus fled with little more than the clothes on their backs. For days, they walked with some neighbors to the refugee camp where they now live. Zahra has no idea when she and her brother will be able to leave the camp. She has no idea where they will go. She was a good student before the war and is grateful for the camp school. Schoolwork is the one thing Zahra feels she can control.

Children orphaned by war in Idlib, Syria. The Orphan Foundation, a Turkish charity, says there are 1.2 million war orphans in Idlib orphanages and camps.

According to the **United Nations** Children's Fund (UNICEF), 36.5 million children in the world have been forced to leave their homes because of conflict. Of those 36.5 million, 13.7 million children are refugees. Another 22.8 million children are internally displaced. Refugees are people who have fled their own countries and crossed a border into another country. Internally displaced people (IDPs) are those who flee their homes to settle someplace safer internally, or in their own countries.

This is an important difference because officially recognized refugees have rights under international law. These rights include legal protections and assistance. IDPs are under the protection of their own government. But it is often their own government that is the cause of the conflict that forced them to flee. This can mean IDPs receive little or no help and remain in very unsafe situations.

A **civil war** has been waged in Syria since 2011. The United Nations (UN) estimates that more than 350,000 civilians have been killed so far in the war. Almost 6 million Syrians have been forced to flee their homes as IDPs or refugees.

# Conflict Situations

**Children live in conflict situations all over the world. Some of that conflict is war—either between countries or within a country. Other forms of conflict include** terrorism, **as well as acts of violence by a government against its own people or between armed gangs and civilians, or people who aren't in the armed forces.**

Wars are one form of armed conflict that occur between two or more different countries. Wars are often fought over territory. For example, one country may want to rule the land of another country to control its wealth and resources. Many wars in history have been waged by empires wanting to expand their power and territory. Empires were groups of territories controlled by single countries.

People living in war zones either have to fight for their own survival, live in destroyed areas, or leave their homes in order to live peacefully somewhere else. These French citizens living in **occupied** Paris during **World War II** (WWII) rose up against their German occupiers and helped Allied forces fight to free France.

## Weapons of War

Wars also happen when disagreements can't be settled. War between countries usually involves official declarations from the governments involved and often the invasion of territory by military forces. These forces use conventional weapons of war, or weapons that do not cause mass destruction. Conventional war may include bombing from the air, shelling, missile or rocket attacks, and the use of armored combat vehicles such as tanks, helicopters, and drones. Weapons are not just aimed at enemy forces. They often target civilian populations, killing and wounding people as well as destroying homes, schools, businesses, and **infrastructure**.

War makes it impossible to live in many cities where food is scarce, water and heating are cut off, and roads and bridges are destroyed. Soldiers and volunteers help Ukrainian civilians escape a bombed-out area in the city of Irpin. The war in Ukraine is an ongoing conflict in the Eastern European country of Ukraine that began when Russia invaded in 2014.

## Rules of War

It may seem odd, but war has "laws" or "rules." Some of these were established over 150 years ago to help protect civilians and the wounded. Swiss businessman Henry Dunant visited an Italian battlefield in 1859 and saw 40,000 wounded and dying soldiers. He was shocked that there was no organized method of care for the wounded. Dunant returned home and helped form what would later become the International Committee of the Red Cross (ICRC). From there, the idea of the Geneva Conventions took root.

Henry Dunant's visit to the Battle of Solferino in Italy led him to write a book and push for laws that safeguarded wounded soldiers after battle. It also led to the founding of the ICRC, an organization that helps civilian victims of war and conflict.

Wounded soldiers wait for care at an American Red Cross first aid station in France during **World War I** (WWI). The Geneva Conventions protect wounded soldiers and those who have surrendered, or laid down their arms.

## The Geneva Conventions

The Geneva Conventions are four international treaties, or agreements, between countries on how soldiers and civilians should be treated during war. The fourth Geneva Convention deals with the treatment of civilians. It was adopted in 1949, four years after the end of World War II. This convention prohibits random attacks on civilians. Among other things, it also states that civilians are to be protected from murder, torture, or **brutality**, and from **discrimination** based on race, nationality, religion, or political opinion.

Firefighters aim their hoses at homes and streets damaged by bombs dropped on London, UK, during World War II. About 50 to 55 million civilians died in WWII.

PERSPECTIVES

Mo won four Olympic gold medals for Britain. He was honored with a knighthood in 2017.

### Mo Farah, War Refugee and Gold Medalist

Sir Mohamed, or Mo, Farah is a very successful British long-distance runner. But until July 2022, not many people knew his true story. Mo was born Hussein Abdi Kahin in 1983 in Somalia, Africa. When he was four, his father was killed in the **Somali civil war**. Mo was separated from his mother. When he was nine, he was told he was going to live with relatives in England. Instead, Mo was given a new name and forced to live with and work for a family he did not know. This is a form of illegally **trafficking** humans. When he was 12, he was allowed to attend school, where he confided in a teacher the truth about his background. That teacher helped to get him removed from the home where he was being held. As an adult, Mo was able to contact his mother in Somalia. She had not known if her son was still alive.

## Civil War

Civil war is a violent conflict within a country that occurs between the government and one or more groups. There have been many civil wars throughout history. They are bloody and leave long-lasting scars because they are fought between citizens of the same country. Civil wars are fought for many reasons, including grievances or greed. A grievance could mean a government's unequal treatment of an **ethnic** or religious group, which leads to armed rebellion against the government and then civil war. Greed could mean two sides fighting over an economic issue, including control over resources such as oil or land. Many civil wars today also grow to involve outside forces, such as other countries and rebel groups from outside of the country.

People become internally displaced as they flee to avoid violence during civil wars. They may also cross borders and become refugees. Displaced by an ongoing civil war in Syria, these children are living in and attending school in camps in Idlib, a city in northern Syria. The camps are not always safe from armed attacks and bombings by government forces.

## American Civil War

The United States experienced a devastating civil war from 1861 to 1865. Around 620,000 Americans died in that war, which is more than the number of American deaths from World War I and World War II combined. In the American Civil War, the northern states, called the Union, fought against the southern states, or the Confederacy. In some cases, friends and family members found themselves on opposite sides of the war.

One of the main issues of that war was slavery, with the northern states wanting to end slavery and southern states wanting to maintain the right to keep humans enslaved. The war created waves of displacement. Many of the displaced were enslaved Black people escaping their captivity. It is estimated that 1 million enslaved people freed themselves during the war, and that 500,000 lived in camps around the United States. Displacements continued after the war.

Self-freed people, who escaped captivity during the Civil War, often presented themselves to the Union Army. In 1861, they were considered "contraband" or captured enemy property. They worked for the Union and were paid a wage.

## State Violence and Genocide

State violence is when a state or government causes deliberate harm and suffering to groups and individuals. It includes genocide, or the intentional destruction of a people on a mass scale. State violence can also mean state **harassment**, terrorism, and police brutality.

The term genocide was first used by Polish-Jewish lawyer Raphael Lemkin in 1944. Lemkin researched mass killings before WWII. He barely escaped being rounded up by the **Nazi regime** in Poland during that war. He lost 49 members of his family in the Holocaust (1941–1945)—the genocide of European Jews by the Nazis. After the war, Lemkin pressured governments into making genocide an internationally recognized crime. In 1948, the United Nations finally adopted the Genocide Convention, a resolution Lemkin wrote. It was a document that defined the crime of genocide.

Lemkin's term genocide combined the ancient Greek and Latin words for "race" and "kill." He wrote many papers on the subject. Genocides always split and destroy families. Survivors of genocide are displaced and often cannot, or do not want to, return to their original homes because of fear.

Images of people murdered in the Holocaust are displayed on a wall at the Holocaust Memorial Museum in Washington, D.C. Entire families and villages were slaughtered by the Nazi regime because of their religion and culture.

## The Armenian Genocide

State violence and genocide aren't new. People, cultures, and ethnic groups all over the world have their own names for this kind of mass slaughter. Lemkin researched many in his quest to have laws made against them. One of these was the 1915 to 1917 mass killings of Armenians in the **Ottoman Empire**. In 1915, Armenians were removed from their homes and made to walk long distances to **concentration camps** in the desert in what is now Syria. These became known as death marches. Between 600,000 to 1 million Armenians died along the way, through exhaustion, starvation, or violence. Armenians call the genocide *Medz Yeghern*, meaning "Great Evil Crime."

Armenian children were deliberately targeted during the genocide. Many were murdered with their families. These Armenian orphans were refugees adopted into Turkish families where many lost their language, culture, and religion. Today, this is known as a form of cultural genocide. This is the intentional destruction of a culture, including beliefs, traditions, and language.

***I became interested in genocide because it happened so many times. It happened to the Armenians and after the Armenians, Hitler took action.***

**Raphael Lemkin**

Most people fleeing gang and criminal violence travel to places of safety within their own countries. Others cross borders seeking refugee status because their own countries cannot keep them safe.

> *Because being aware of what is happening in our era and choosing to do nothing about it has become unacceptable. Because we cannot allow ourselves to go on normalizing horror and violence. Because we can all be held accountable if something happens under our noses and we don't dare even look.*
>
> **VALERIA LUISELLI,**
> **AUTHOR OF *TELL ME HOW IT ENDS***

## Gang Conflict and Violence

Millions of people around the world are forced to leave their homes because of the violence of criminal gangs. This violence rages in the neighborhoods of cities and villages and makes their streets unsafe. Children in these neighborhoods are at risk of being recruited into the gangs. They are also targets if they don't join gangs. They are unable to have normal lives free of fear.

Some parents are forced to make the difficult decision to save their children by sending them away alone. When they arrive at an international border, these children are called unaccompanied minors. Most unaccompanied minors arriving at borders are teenagers, but some are as young as six or seven years old. The journey itself holds many dangers, including the possibility of being trafficked. There is a possibility that these children may be deported, or forced to return, after reaching a new country.

Unaccompanied minors from Central America wait to be processed at the U.S. border. By the time the children reach the border, they have undergone long and often dangerous journeys.

## Recognition as Migrants

The United Nations High Commissioner for Refugees (UNHCR) is the United Nations' refugee agency. Starting in 2010, it produced information for people fleeing to other countries because of criminal gang violence. It outlined who might be victims of gang violence and why. People who resist or oppose gang activity are at risk—both children and adults. Children who refuse to be recruited are at risk, as well as adolescent girls who refuse sexual demands by gangs. Children may be lured into gangs by promises of money and status. They are also threatened into joining with beatings, sexual assaults, and kidnappings.

The UNHCR believes gang violence is as dangerous to children as war. According to the Norwegian Refugee Council, around 600,000 people were internally displaced by gang violence in Central America in 2021 alone. In Haiti, 96,000 people were internally displaced by gang violence in the country's capital, Port-au-Prince. When people can't find safety within their own countries, they make longer journeys on foot, by boat, or by bus to the borders of countries where they believe they will be safe.

For parents in countries such as El Salvador, Honduras, Guatemala, and Mexico, the United States represents safety for their children. Many believe a child arriving at the border alone has a better chance of being admitted to the country than if a whole family arrives together.

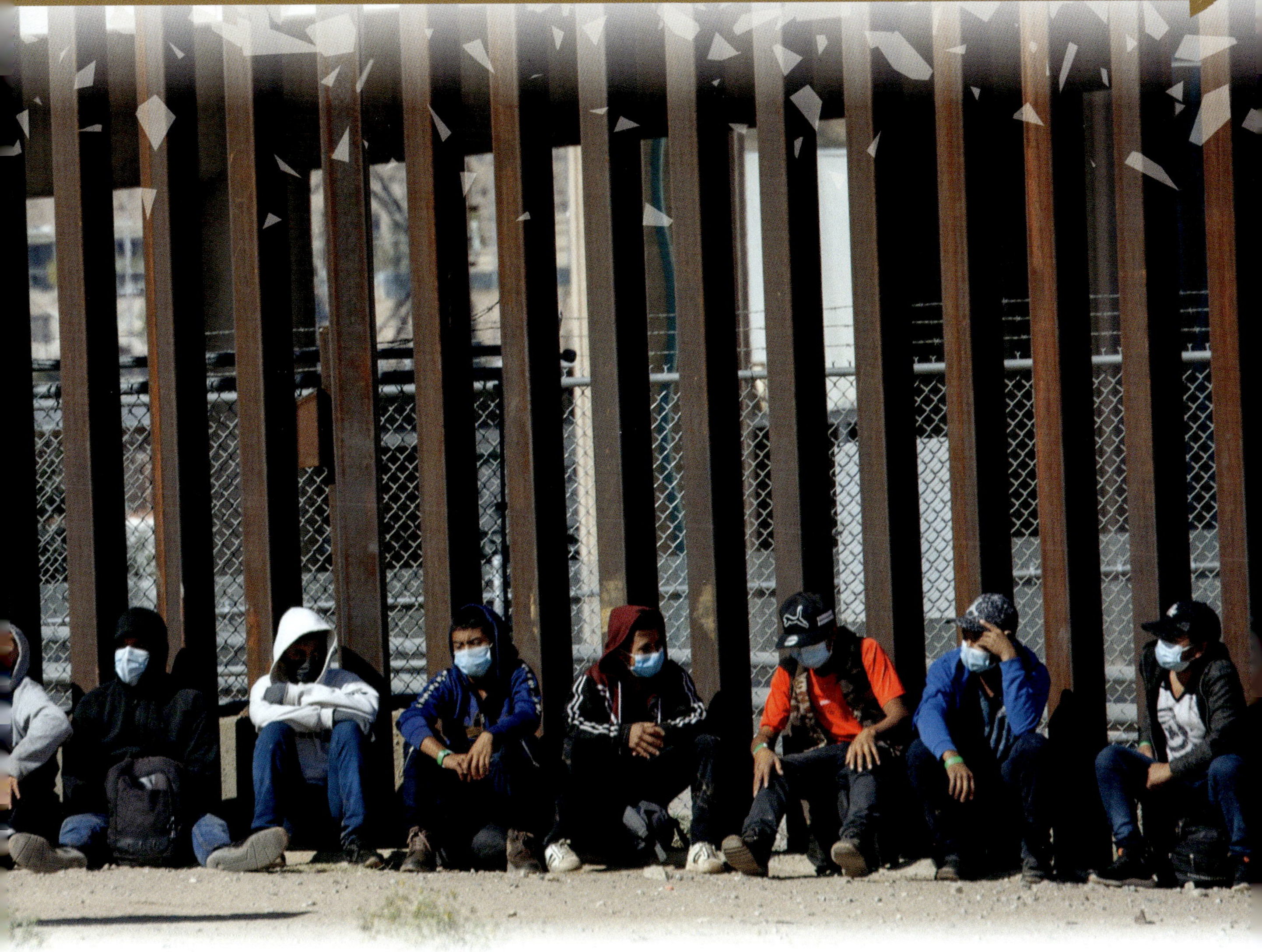

A group of migrants surrender to U.S. border patrol in Mexico. When a child arrives at the U.S. border, he or she is detained in a government facility. The government must then arrange safe shelter while the court system decides whether the child can legally stay in the country.

## CONSIDER THIS

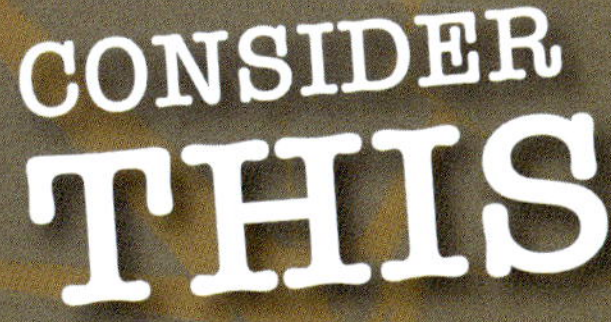

What are the similarities and differences between refugees leaving their countries to escape war and migrants leaving their countries to escape gang violence? How do these similarities and differences affect how they are perceived or treated?

## Chapter Two

German children watch as U.S. tanks enter their town during the end of World War II. The Rights of the Child recognizes that children's rights are not conditional, or dependent upon anything such as wealth, race, or where they come from. It recognizes that children are not the property of their parents or their government.

# Rights of Children and Refugees

**"Someone who is unable or unwilling to return to their country of origin owing to a well-founded fear of being** persecuted **for reasons of race, religion, nationality, membership of a particular social group, or political opinion." This is the internationally recognized definition of a refugee, as stated in the 1951 Refugee Convention—an important legal document and an indicator of how refugees, including children, were viewed and assisted in a post-World War era.**

In World War I (1914–1918), 12 million people were displaced from their homes, and during World War II (1939–1945), 60 million were displaced. Civilians were heavily targeted during these wars. Record amounts of people had to flee their homes to avoid being killed. For children, these experiences were devastating and **traumatic**. The Declaration of the Rights of the Child, written by Eglantyne Jebb, was supported by the **League of Nations** in 1924 and expanded by the United Nations in 1946 after WWII. Today, the declaration is known as the United Nations Convention on the Rights of the Child (UNCRC). It is an international treaty that outlines the many rights children have, including the right to live in safety.

PERSPECTIVES

Jebb's work became a key part in how children's rights are understood and protected today.

## Eglantyne Jebb, Child Rights Advocate

Eglantyne Jebb (1876–1928) was a British social reformer, or a person who worked to change society. After WWI, she heard reports of how children in Germany and Austria-Hungary were starving due to the damages of war. She was moved by the suffering of these children. As a result, Jebb set up the Save the Children Fund (now Save the Children) in 1919 to provide emergency aid to children during conflicts and disasters. She also wrote the Declaration of the Rights of the Child, a document promoting child rights, in 1923.

In any era, conflict creates civilian victims—often for decades after the conflict ends. These French women and children are walking in the ruins of their city after World War I. It took more than 15 years for parts of Europe to rebuild after that war.

## Rights Reinforced

Even with the Geneva Conventions and the Declaration of the Rights of the Child, children in conflict zones are vulnerable. In 1989, the United Nations adopted the Convention on the Rights of the Child, with 196 countries signing up since then. The UNCRC defines children as being under 18, unless stated otherwise by their countries of origin. It notes that children have the right to protections. Some of those protections include the right to seek refugee status according to law and to receive humanitarian assistance. Children make up about one-third of the world's population. However, by the end of 2021 they made up more than 40 percent of the world's refugees.

The high number of child refugees and IDPs is due in part to the difficult decisions often made by parents to send their children to safety. This has also been true in history. During WWII, children were evacuated and displaced from their homes in London, UK, and sent to the countryside over fears of German bombing. Called Operation Pied Piper, it was traumatic for children who were separated from their parents amidst the fear of an enemy invasion.

## Who Are They?

Migrant, asylum seeker, internally displaced person, refugee, forcibly displaced person—there are so many terms used to describe people fleeing desperate situations that it can get confusing. Migrant is a basic term that describes someone who has moved away from their usual home. Asylum seekers are people who have left their country and are looking for protection from persecution or threats to their life. Internally displaced people have been forced to leave their homes but still remain living in their home countries. Refugees are people unable to stay in their own country because they fear persecution based on a number of defined categories. Forcibly displaced is a term that includes refugees, asylum seekers, and other people in need of international protection.

Haitian migrants cross the border from Mexico to seek asylum in the United States in 2021. Many of these people had earlier settled in Brazil and Chile after fleeing targeted gang violence in Haiti. When those countries expelled them, they made their way to the U.S. border. There, they were then forced onto flights back to Haiti, where gang violence still threatened them.

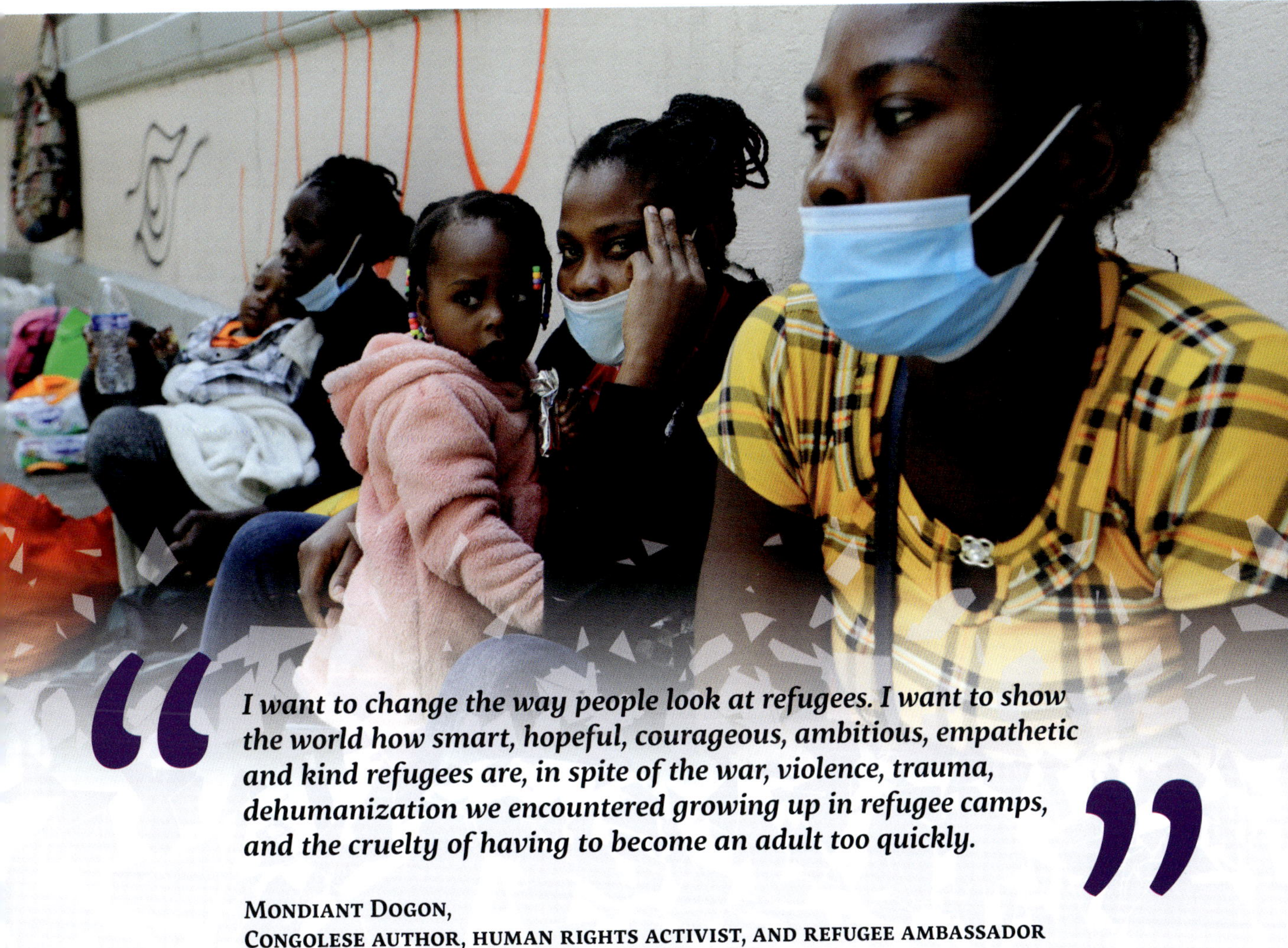

> ***I want to change the way people look at refugees. I want to show the world how smart, hopeful, courageous, ambitious, empathetic and kind refugees are, in spite of the war, violence, trauma, dehumanization we encountered growing up in refugee camps, and the cruelty of having to become an adult too quickly.***
>
> **Mondiant Dogon,**
> **Congolese author, human rights activist, and refugee ambassador**

## Desperate Journeys

They don't want to be standing on the shore of the Mediterranean Sea, waiting to climb into a rubber boat. They know how risky the journey is. Some have paid as much as $3,500 for their seat. For their money, they may or may not be given a life jacket to wear. The boat is likely in very bad shape and might not have enough fuel to reach the Italian coast. There is a good chance that the smugglers will abandon the boat at sea or that the boat will capsize. But life back home was so bad that this is the better option.

In 2015, more than 1 million refugees crossed the Mediterranean Sea to reach Europe, with 3,771 reported dead or missing. In 2021, 123,300 crossings were reported, but 3,231 were reported dead or missing. The UNHCR is worried that while the number of crossings is decreasing, the percentage of deaths on these crossings is increasing.

Smugglers are the people refugees pay if they need help on their journey. Smugglers often take advantage of desperate people and put their lives at risk by crowding too many people into boats to make as much money as they can. Some smugglers have faced fines and imprisonment for their disregard for human life.

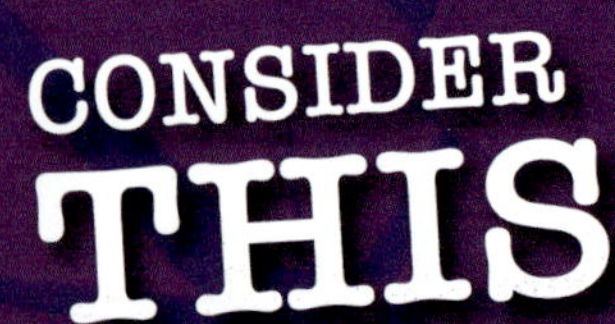


The UNCRC states that decisions affecting the life of a child must be in his or her best interest. Does a family's decision to flee across the Mediterranean Sea meet this standard? Why or why not?

PERSPECTIVES

## Alan Kurdi, Child Migrant

It has often been said that a picture is worth a thousand words. Alan Kurdi was only two years old when he drowned in the Mediterranean Sea with his mother and brother. They were Syrian refugees, trying to escape civil war and build a new life in Canada. On September 2, 2015, Alan and his family boarded a rubber boat. There were 16 people in the boat, but it was only meant for eight people. It capsized after just a few minutes and several people on board drowned. The world might never have known Alan's name, but there was a photographer on the beach when his small, lifeless body washed up on shore. The picture of Alan's body caused outcry around the world. Everyone said more must be done to help refugees. But it was too late for Alan Kurdi.

This mural in Frankfurt, Germany, depicts the photo taken of Alan Kurdi on the beach. Alan and his family had hoped to join relatives in British Columbia, Canada. Alan's aunt, Tima Kurdi, later wrote a book called *The Boy on the Beach*. It detailed the Kurdi family's efforts to escape Syria.

## Asylum Seekers and Refugee Status

The Kurdi family was among the millions of people who have fled their countries without official refugee status. A person hoping to enter a new country as a refugee must first apply for refugee status. Each country has its own process to legally accept refugees. These processes are often complicated and take a long time. They can be extremely difficult for people to navigate, often without the help of lawyers. These factors often lead to people choosing to seek asylum. This means they enter another country to ask for protection and to be recognized as a refugee. Seeking asylum is a legal human right.

For children seeking refugee status, the rules are sometimes different. This is especially true for unaccompanied children, or those who have been separated from or lost their parents. In Canada, for example, refugee status claims by unaccompanied children are given priority and children are assigned a representative who will act in their best interest. The United States provides long-term assistance to unaccompanied refugee children through the Unaccompanied Refugee Minors (URM) Program.

Article 22 of the UNCRC recognizes the right of refugee children to receive special protection. It notes that refugee children are vulnerable and need the protection and support of adults.

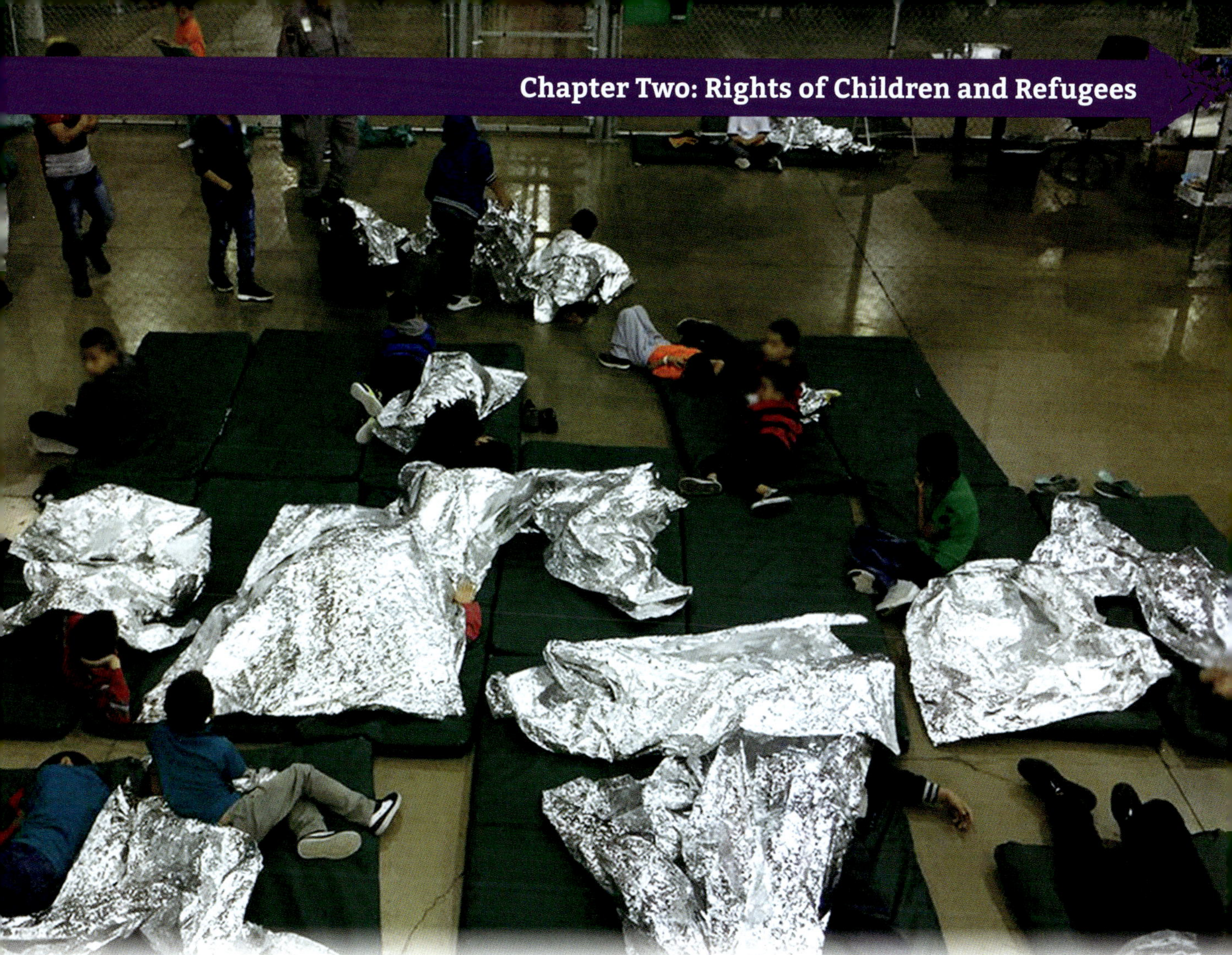

These children sleep on mats in a detention facility for immigrants in Texas. They have been separated from their parents. It was later revealed that there was not a system in place to ensure the children and parents were reunited.

## Separated at the Border

From April to June 2018, when asylum seekers arrived at the United States border, families were separated and kept in different detention facilities. It is estimated that 5,500 children and infants were taken from their parents at the border. Some people supported this action, saying that it was necessary to stop people from showing up at the border without going through the proper application process to enter the country. But this process was not an option for many of these refugees. The court system stopped the practice and ordered that families be reunified, or brought back together. But many parents had already been deported. In 2021, it was reported that more than 1,700 children had not yet been reunited with their families.

Chapter Three

# Displaced in a Conflict Zone

**Every year, conflicts displace more people across the globe—89.3 million at the end of 2021. Most are internally displaced people, who resettle temporarily or permanently in safer areas of their own country. IDPs account for 53.2 million people. Of those, 22.8 million are children.**

For children displaced in conflict zones, the constant threat of violence becomes normal. In an ongoing conflict situation, such as the Syrian civil war that began in 2011, people are often repeatedly displaced from their homes and temporary shelters. Conflict becomes part of everyday life. Soldiers or armed fighters patrol streets. Schools and hospitals are attacked, disrupting education and health care. Children are abducted, targeted in attacks, and recruited as child soldiers. Fear is constant.

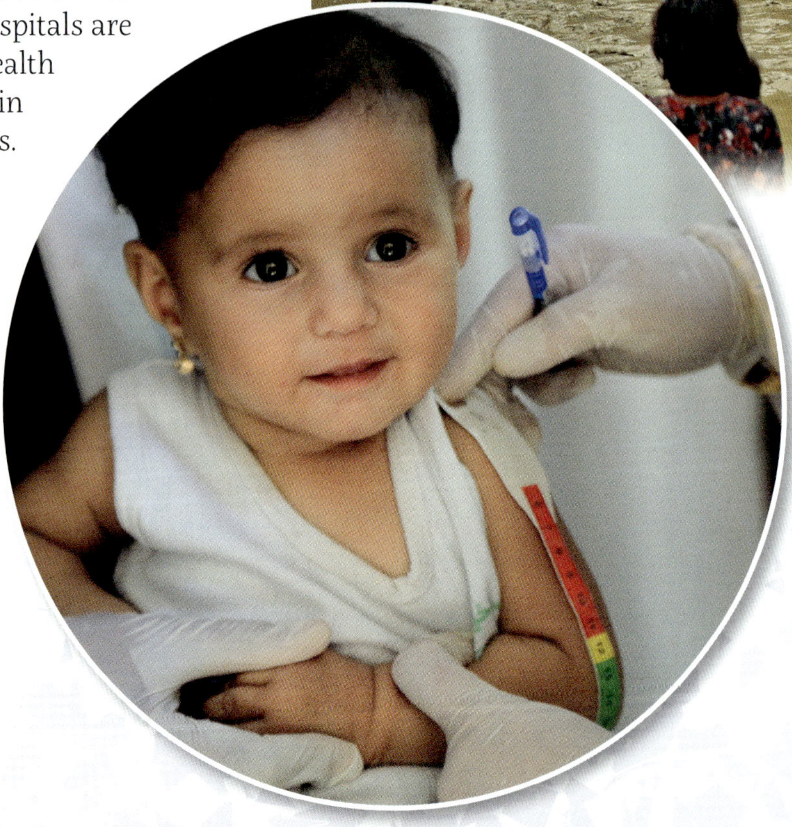

Because food, clean water, and medical care are difficult to access, children in conflict zones suffer more from diseases. Here, a doctor examines a Syrian baby to measure for malnutrition. This is the condition that happens when a person's diet does not contain enough nutrients.

## The Challenges of Statelessness

Refugees may wait for many years before they are accepted in a new country. IDPs face the challenge of having fewer rights under international law than those with refugee status. And there are some groups of people who receive almost no government protections. Millions of people are stateless, which means that no country considers them citizens. They may be unable to access basic rights, such as health care, in the countries where they live. When stateless people are displaced due to violence, they are extra vulnerable. Without citizenship documents, it can be difficult to access international help or protection.

The Rohingya were denied citizenship by their home country of Myanmar in 1982, where they are a Muslim minority group. When more than 1 million Rohingya fled the country during the **Rohingya genocide**, beginning in 2016, they were not internationally recognized as refugees due to their statelessness. In Bangladesh, where most fled, a lack of refugee status means there are few protections and opportunities for work and education.

## Ethiopia

In 2021, Ethiopia had 5.1 million IDPs, the highest number ever recorded by a country in a single year. A civil war began in Ethiopia's northern Tigray Region in November 2020 between the Ethiopian government and its allies, and the Tigray People's Liberation Front (TPLF), a political party. All sides committed extremely cruel acts. Civilians were targeted in attacks on schools, health care facilities, and temporary shelters. At the same time, Ethiopia has also been experiencing a drought, or a long period with little or no rain. This is causing more people to leave their homes. Children are extremely vulnerable. As they flee, they are in danger of facing violent attacks and other abuses, or being trafficked.

In 2022, the Ethiopian government declared a truce with forces in Tigray. Hundreds of thousands of IDPs have returned to their communities. However, many now face the destruction of their homes and a lack of infrastructure, services, and education. It was estimated in 2023 that more than 3.4 million Ethiopian children do not have access to school.

Protesters speak out in New York City in 2021 against the Ethiopian government's actions. That year, the UN stated that the Ethiopian government was using **famine** as a weapon of war. It prevented aid organizations from getting food and supplies to people in Tigray, where the TPLF is in control.

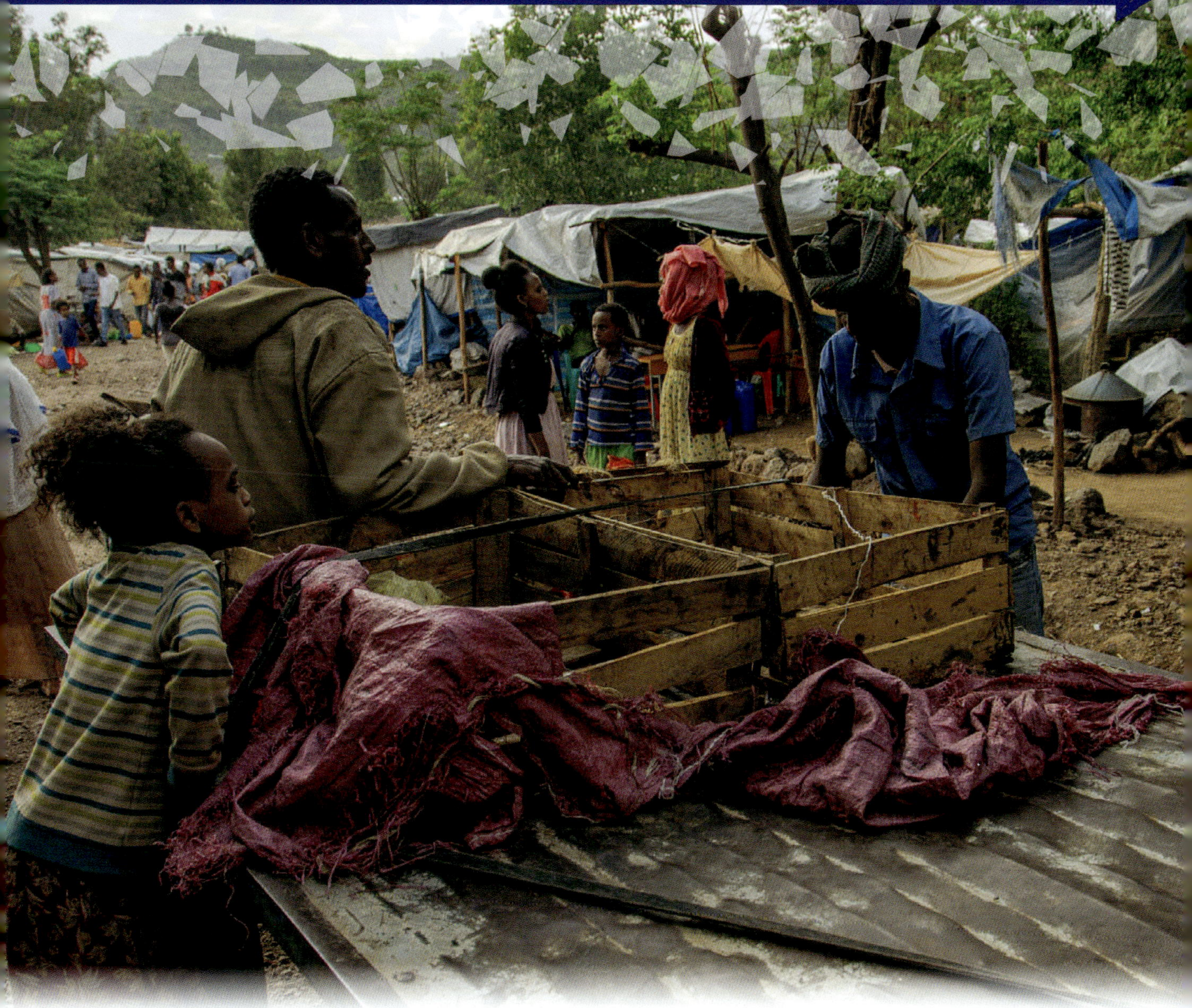

Many people were displaced repeatedly throughout the Ethiopian civil war. Though some have returned to their communities, a large number of Ethiopian IDPs and refugees have been unable to return. Many fear violence from troops still in the area and wonder if peace will be short-lived.

**CONSIDER THIS**

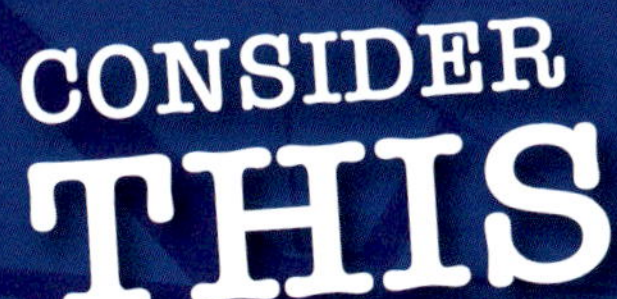

Why do you think statistics about child refugees and IDPs often note the lack of access to education? How is the right to education of particular importance for children?

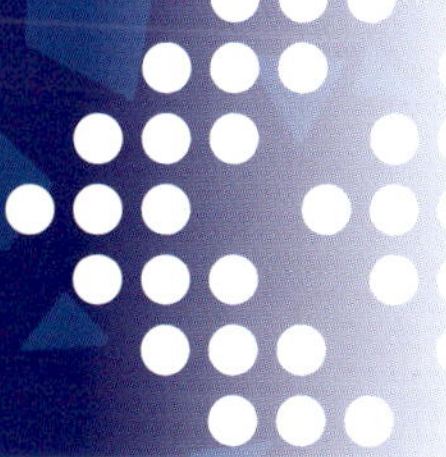

A Palestinian child stands up to Israeli soldiers in the West Bank, part of the remaining Palestinian territory.

## Palestine

Since the creation of Israel in 1948, Israelis and Palestinians have fought several wars over land. Both sides claim a right to the land for historical and religious reasons. When Israel was created, a nine-month war followed that ended with Israel controlling large areas that were previously part of Palestine. The Palestinians were massively displaced. Most became refugees, leaving their homes for surrounding areas such as Lebanon, Syria, and Jordan. Some are IDPs, still living in Palestinian territories that are occupied by Israel's military.

It is estimated that there are hundreds of thousands of IDPs in Israeli-occupied Palestine. More Palestinians are displaced every year due to the ongoing conflict.

## Generations of Displacement

Since this massive displacement, generations of Palestinians have been born as refugees and IDPs. This means that most Palestinians are stateless, and don't have the protections that come along with citizenship, nor are they able to gain official refugee status. Many Palestinian refugee children grow up in and attend school in refugee camps.

There have been violent attacks on these camps and schools and children have died. The United Nations created a separate aid organization to care for Palestinian refugees. It is known as the United Nations Relief and Works Agency for Palestinian Refugees in the Near East (UNRWA). When it began in 1950, it assisted 750,000 Palestinians. Today, there are 5.9 million Palestinians eligible for UNWRA services.

More than 5.6 million Palestinians are registered with UNRWA as refugees. More than half of them are children.

> ***Palestine is my homeland. [...] But when I think with reason, what am I going to do there? I've never been there. If I go to Palestine I will be a stranger.***
>
> **MOHAMMAD, PALESTINIAN REFUGEE BORN IN JORDAN, INTERVIEW IN *+972 MAGAZINE*, FEBRUARY 2014**

## Ukraine

In February 2022, Russia invaded Ukraine. Russia has committed hundreds of war crimes, such as crimes against humanity, and violated international laws of war. By refusing to formally declare war, however, Russia attempts to justify its actions. After one month of war, more than half of Ukraine's 7.5 million children were displaced. There are 6.5 million IDPs in Ukraine and more than 8 million refugees across Europe.

It has been reported that Russian troops have sent thousands of Ukrainian children to Russia for adoption as part of a massive deportation program. Some of the children were separated from their families and some were living in orphanages. Without families to protect them, orphaned children who are displaced are especially vulnerable. There has been international anger over these reports, which Russia says are not true.

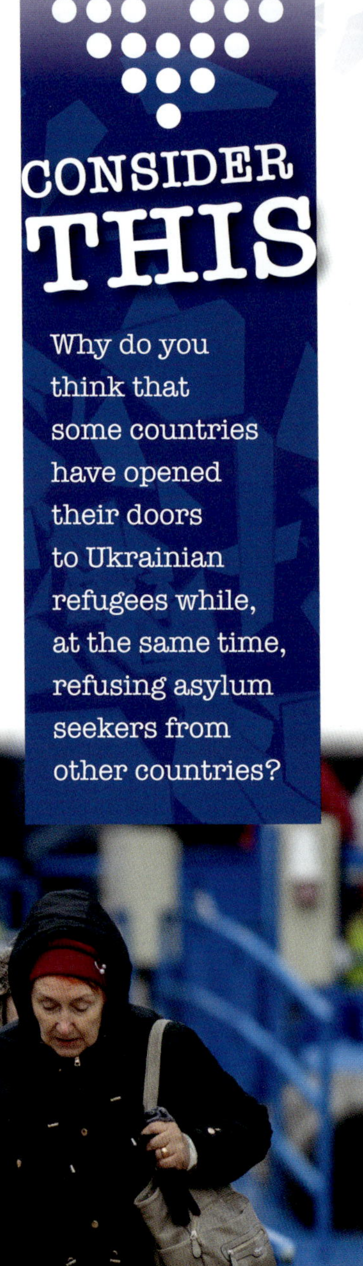

CONSIDER THIS

Why do you think that some countries have opened their doors to Ukrainian refugees while, at the same time, refusing asylum seekers from other countries?

Canada, the United States, and many European countries have opened their doors to Ukrainian refugees. Some experts have pointed out, however, that refugees fleeing similar situations in countries in Africa and the Middle East, such as those fleeing the **Taliban** in Afghanistan, have not been as readily accepted.

PERSPECTIVES

## Children with Disabilities

Around one in five internally displaced people in Ukraine have developmental delays or disabilities. Ukrainian children with disabilities who had been living in care facilities are suffering greatly from the effects of the war. Thousands of them were sent home at the beginning of the war without any assessment if their home environment was safe for them. Many of these children are no longer receiving medical treatment. For the children who are still in care facilities, some of them have been displaced to other facilities around the country, and their families often don't know where they are. These children also run the risk of experiencing neglect and abuse when sent to unknown facilities.

Safely evacuating children with disabilities can be extremely difficult and sometimes impossible due to a lack of **accessible** transportation, shelter, and services. Often, children with disabilities are not included in evacuation plans when wars first begin.

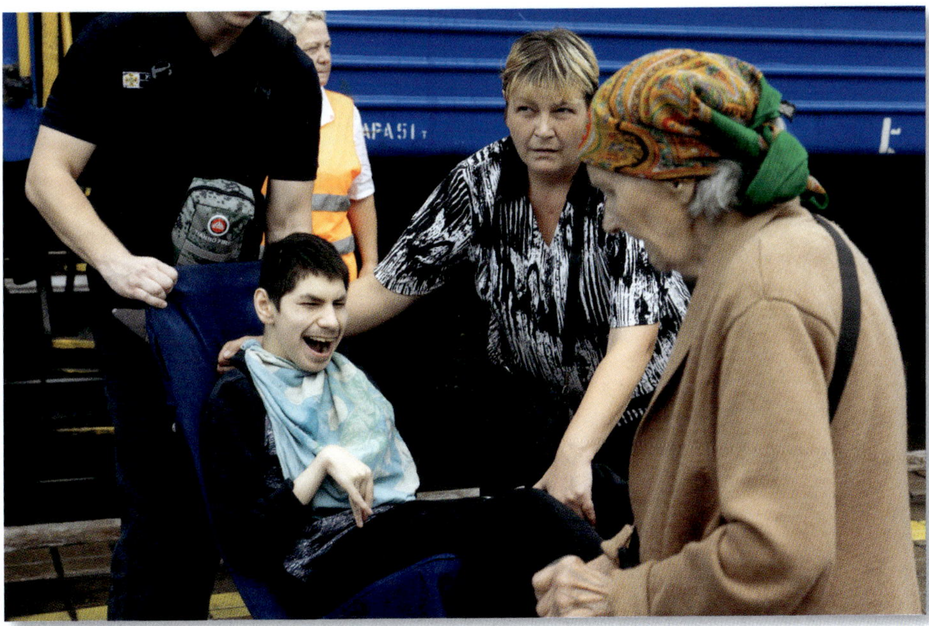

> ***Too often invisible, too often forgotten, and too often overlooked, refugees with disabilities are among the most isolated, socially excluded and marginalized of all displaced populations.***
>
> **António Guterres,**
> **Secretary-General of the United Nations**

Chapter Four

# Protecting Child Refugees

**Refugees and asylum seekers have rights under international law. Children, too, have universal rights that are recognized by the United Nations. But these rights aren't always protected. There are still millions of child refugees around the world seeking safety and protection. Many organizations and people are working to change this.**

International organizations agree that child refugees are particularly vulnerable. They may be separated from their families. They experience violence, abuse, and neglect. They may be trafficked or forced into child marriages. Many deal with mental illnesses, isolation, and discrimination as they attempt to navigate their new lives or find safety.

UNICEF has a range of initiatives that address these challenges. One aim is to give families the tools to protect themselves, such as learning ways to obtain legal advice. Another is to provide response services such as therapy, legal aid, and emergency financial assistance. Organizations such as Kids in Need of Defense (KIND) also provide free legal aid to unaccompanied children.

## Gender-Based Violence

UNICEF initiatives also aim to protect children from gender-based violence. Women and girls are often at particular risk of having their rights violated in times of conflict, from being denied the right to education to being subjected to sexual violence or forced into slavery or child marriages. However, boys can also experience sexual violence. UNICEF programs focus on providing survivors with health services, mental health and social support, and information on how to access aid and where to report abuse.

(left) An important goal of UNICEF and other aid organizations is to reunify unaccompanied children with their families.

(below) One way UNICEF tackles gender-based violence is by empowering women and girls through economic and social initiatives. This includes providing tuition for children to attend school and offering business leadership and financial literacy programs for women.

## Resettlement

Refugees may move many times before they settle permanently. They may have spent years in refugee camps, waiting to return home or be accepted into a new country. The Dadaab refugee camps in Kenya provide shelter for hundreds of thousands of refugees, many of whom escaped conflict and drought in Somalia. But safety there is unstable. The Kenyan government has pushed for some refugees to return to their countries. In 2021, it ordered the camps to be closed. Amidst international pressure, this closure has been delayed and two camps have been reopened. Some refugees who returned to Somalia have now come back to Dadaab. Life for them is still in limbo.

### CONSIDER THIS

Should refugee camps be considered long-term solutions for those fleeing danger in their countries? Why or why not?

Open since 1991, the overcrowded Dadaab camps are the only homes some child refugees have known. They live with the constant stress that their homes may be taken away.

Each year, more refugees are in need of resettlement.

## Long-Term Solutions

Many organizations are focused on long-term settlement for refugees. The International Bar Association argues that it is time to change the long legal process required to be accepted as a refugee. It proposes that Emergency Evacuation Visas (EEVs) could ensure that refugees can quickly reach safety. Then, with government support, they can decide on the resettlement pathway that is right for them. RefugePoint is an organization focused on finding long-term solutions for refugees. It created a resettlement program that has partnered with the UN Refugee Agency to assist refugees in accessing resettlement opportunities. It has helped more than 100,000 refugees access pathways to safety.

At the Māngere Refugee Resettlement Centre, refugees can access a range of services, such as English-language classes and mental health support, to help them better prepare for their new lives in New Zealand.

According to the American Psychiatric Association, an average of one in three refugees deals with mental health challenges, such as post-traumatic stress, depression, and anxiety. The World Health Organization (WHO) states that more support for them is needed.

## Healing the Scars of Conflict

Child refugees have been robbed of their childhood. They have been placed in incredibly unsafe situations and forced to witness things that children should never have to face. Refugee children develop scars. They may or may not have physical scars, but emotional scars are always there. At the same time, child refugees are resilient. With support from their communities, they can find ways to cope and thrive.

The National Child Traumatic Stress Network (NCTSN) is an American agency that is dedicated to helping children and their families who witness or experience traumatic events. It describes different types of stress that can affect refugee children, even after they are safely resettled. Traumatic stress, for example, comes from a child's experiences during the conflict, while resettlement stress occurs as refugee children try to create a life in their new country. Knowing about these stresses can help others provide much-needed support to child refugees.

PERSPECTIVES

From a refugee to governor general, Michaëlle's story has inspired many, and proves that the scars of conflict, while never fully gone, can certainly be overcome.

## Michaëlle Jean, Refugee to Governor General

Michaëlle Jean was born in Haiti in 1957. Soon after, the Haitian government became a dictatorship, and soldiers used violence and murder against anyone who spoke against the government. Michaëlle's father, who was a principal and a teacher, was arrested and tortured. The family knew it was time to leave Haiti. They came to Canada in 1968 and were granted refugee status. Michaëlle has spoken about the trauma she felt as a schoolchild in Canada. She described being "silent and withdrawn." However, with the support and encouragement of a teacher, she had the courage to share her experiences. Michaëlle earned university degrees and worked at the Canadian Broadcasting Corporation (CBC). Then, in 2005, she was appointed as the governor general of Canada, which is the representative of the British **monarch** in Canada.

***[My teacher] asked me to share my experience with my classmates. When she did so, she gave me a voice that helped me unpack some very troublesome and painful memories. [...] Her generous attitude changed my life.***

MICHAËLLE JEAN

## The Importance of Being Seen

One of the dangers that child refugees face is the belief that they don't matter. Children depend on adults to protect and care for them. When children are put into dangerous and traumatic situations, they are being betrayed and harmed by adults—sending the harmful and untrue message that their lives are unimportant. It is important that traumatized children understand that they matter, that they are seen, and that they are heard.

(above) A family welcomes the first Syrian refugees to Canada in December 2015.

Programs focused on welcoming child refugees into their new communities can help show them that they are valued and important. Every summer, the International Rescue Committee hosts a five-week program for newly arrived child refugees in New York. The program aims to build the children's confidence and self-esteem, provide them with essential support networks, and prepare them for school in their new country.

(below) In some countries, volunteer programs pair citizens with refugees to help welcome them into new communities and access the services they need. These programs can also help promote friendship and a sharing of cultures.

The name Amal means hope in Arabic.

## Little Amal

A unique project aims to inspire hope and compassion for refugee children around the world. "Little Amal," a 12-foot (3.7 m) puppet, represents a 10-year-old Syrian refugee. She has traveled more than 5,500 miles (9,000 km) across 13 countries. Little Amal reminds the world not to forget about child refugees. At the same time, she represents that child refugees have a lot of potential and can make valuable contributions to their communities.

***I am not just a refugee. I am a human being with dreams, goals and aspirations.***

**Foni Joyce,**
**Former child refugee from South Sudan**

## CONSIDER THIS

What message do you think Foni Joyce is trying to get across? Does her message relate to the message of Little Amal? How can you apply this message when you learn about child refugees?

# Preventing Conflicts

**The best way to prevent children from becoming refugees is to prevent conflicts from happening in the first place. Different international agencies and governments have varying ideas about how best to tackle conflict prevention.**

The United Nations relies on **diplomacy** to encourage peace between nations. It says that conflicts can be resolved through negotiation. The World Economic Forum recommends a "firm but flexible" principle when negotiating between countries on the brink of conflict. Compromise, it states, is the best way to stop conflict from starting.

Without international cooperation, a world without conflict cannot be achieved. In addition to carrying out its initiatives to achieve international peace, such as peacekeeping missions, the UN brings together countries in regular meetings to address threats to peace and security.

## CONSIDER THIS

Where can you learn more about what your country is doing to prevent future conflicts? Why should this information be important to you?

Countries such as the United States and Canada, as well as the United Nations (left), carry out peacekeeping missions around the world. They send officers and experts to help prevent violence, protect civilians, and assist in stopping conflicts and restoring safe communities. An essential part of their work is also to collaborate with local peacekeepers to create long-term solutions.

### North American Strategies

The United States government has issued a report called *The U.S. Strategy to Prevent Conflict and Promote Stability*. The strategy aims to use data and diplomacy to better understand the local politics of the country on the brink of conflict, how best to take action, and how to hold actors responsible. It also focuses on working with governments and organizations for long-term stability. In Canada, the Peace and Stabilization Operations Program supports conflict prevention and global peace. It helps fund and support peacebuilding initiatives and organizations.

## Youth and Peacebuilding

Children represent the future. So who better to have at the table when it comes to peacebuilding? Peacebuilding is the process of ending conflict through nonviolent actions. To encourage more young people to become involved in peacebuilding, the United Nations and other agencies have prepared a report called *Guiding Principles on Young People's Participation in Peacebuilding.* It recognizes that young people can be important drivers of change. A UNICEF peacebuilding program encourages young people to connect with each other to build **solidarity**. One example of the program's work is to train young peer educators, who speak to other young people in their communities about issues that affect them.

UNICEF's peacebuilding program brings together youth from different backgrounds to promote unity. It carries out initiatives in countries around the world, such as Ukraine, Cameroon, Burundi, and Chad.

> ***We believe that children and young people are among the most powerful agents of peace.***
>
> **Catherine Russell,**
> **Executive Director of UNICEF**

PERSPECTIVES

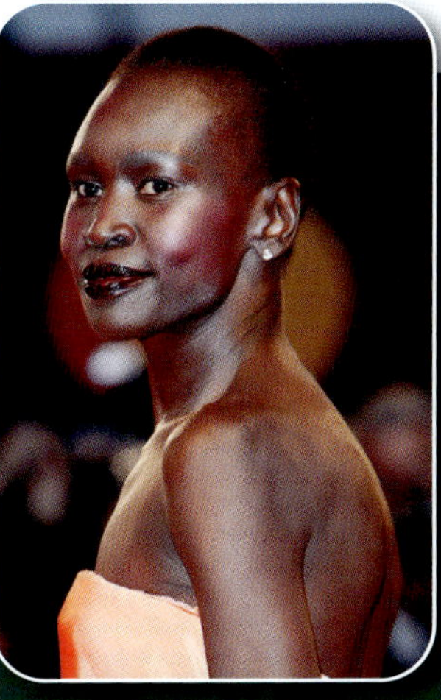

Alek uses her global platform to advocate for refugees and raise awareness about the work being done to help them.

## Alek Wek, Refugee to Model and Spokesperson

Alek was born in 1977 in South Sudan, the seventh of nine children. She describes her African childhood as simple, happy, and beautiful. But that all changed in 1985, when civil war broke out. Alek and her family fled to England when she was 14. When she was 18 she was discovered by a modeling scout. In 1997, she was the first Black model to appear on the cover of *Elle* magazine and she was named Model of the Year by MTV. Alek now works with aid organizations such as UNHCR and Doctors Without Borders. Alek is a supporter of UNHCR's Stand #WithRefugees petition, which calls on governments to ensure every refugee child gets an education and that every refugee family has somewhere safe to live.

These children take part in an event for Refugee Week in the United Kingdom. Raising awareness can be an important tool for youth to get involved. June is World Refugee Awareness Month.

# GLOSSARY

**accessible** Able to be reached or used

**brutality** Extreme cruelty and violence

**civil war** A war between citizens of the same country

**concentration camps** Mass detention camps where many people were killed

**diplomacy** Maintaining peaceful relationships between countries

**discrimination** Unjust treatment because of differences such as gender, ethnicity, and age

**ethnic** Relating to a group of people with a shared cultural background

**famine** Severe food scarcity

**harassment** Persistent behavior that demeans or causes suffering

**infrastructure** The systems and services, such as roads and power plants, that help a society operate

**League of Nations** An international organization formed after WWI; the predecessor to the United Nations

**monarch** A person who rules over a country or empire, such as a queen

**Nazi regime** The fascist government that ruled Germany from 1933 to 1945

**occupied** Taken and controlled by a foreign military

**Ottoman Empire** A large empire established by Turkish tribes around 1300 that ruled for over 600 years

**persecuted** To be treated unfairly or with hostility because of ethnicity or who you are

**Rohingya genocide** The ongoing persecution and killings of Muslim Rohingya people in Myanmar, perpetrated by the Myanmar military

**solidarity** A feeling of unity between people based on shared goals and interests

**Somali civil war** An ongoing civil war in Somalia that began in 1988, leading up to the overthrow of government in 1991 and the fight for power that followed

**Taliban** An extremist Islamic and nationalist group that controlled most of Afghanistan from 1996 to 2001 and took control again in 2021

**terrorism** The illegal use of violence or intimidation for a political purpose

**trafficking** Buying and selling something illegally. Human trafficking is the crime of recruiting, transporting, and forcing a person to provide some kind of labor.

**traumatic** Emotionally upsetting and painful

**United Nations** The international organization formed after WWII that aims to maintain global peace and tackle global issues

**World War I** A global war that was fought between 1914 and 1918

**World War II** A global war that was fought between 1939 and 1945

STAY INFORMED

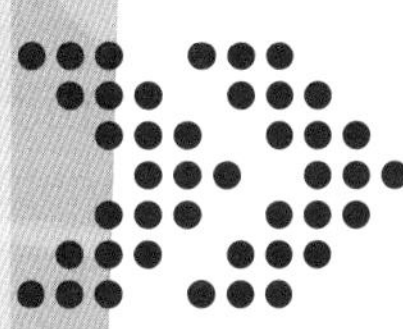

## Child War Refugees and You

More than 450 million children around the world, or one in six, live in a conflict zone. Even though they are less than one-third of the global population, children are more than 40 percent of the world's refugees. What have you learned about the reasons children are displaced and the supports needed for child war refugees and IDPs? What can you do to help child war refugees?

1 Read and learn more about wars and conflicts and how they affect us today.

2 Understand how conflicts and wars displace children and the risks children face when they are displaced.

3 Learn what your country and aid organizations are doing to help child war refugees and IDPs.

4 Share what you have learned with other people.

## Books to Read

Brown, Don. *The Unwanted: Stories of the Syrian Refugees.* Clarion Books, 2018.

Leaving My Homeland and Leaving My Homeland: After the Journey series. Crabtree Publishing, 2017–2020.

Yousafzai, Malala. *We are Displaced: My Journey and Stories from Refugee Girls Around the World.* Little, Brown Books for Young Readers, 2019.

## Websites to Visit

**https://www.thirteen.org/programs/thirteen-specials/refugee-kids-one-small-school-takes-on-the-world-eftfat/**

This short film, *Refugee Kids: One Small School Takes on the World,* chronicles the International Rescue Committee's summer program in New York City, and tells the stories of some of the child refugees involved in the program.

**https://www.unhcr.org/children.html**

Read the stories of child refugees and learn about the challenges they face and the work the UN is doing to support them.

**https://www.unicef.org/emergencies/peacebuilding-social-cohesion**

Explore the links on this page to see UNICEF's youth peacebuilding initiatives in action, from soccer matches in Cameroon to conflict resolution in Ukraine.

# INDEX

## About the Author


**Petrice Custance is a writer and editor. It is her honor to share the stories of incredible children, both past and present, who have shown such courage in the darkest of times.**